At Grandma and Grandpa's House

Ruth Hooker

Illustrations by Ruth Rosner

Albert Whitman & Company, *Niles, Illinois*

Text © 1986 by Ruth Hooker
Illustrations © 1986 by Ruth Rosner
Published in 1986 by Albert Whitman & Company, Niles, Illinois
Published simultaneously in Canada by General Publishing, Limited, Toronto.
All rights reserved. Printed in U.S.A.
10 9 8 7 6 5 4 3 2 1

Library of Congress Cataloging-in-Publication Data

Hooker, Ruth.
    At Grandma and Grandpa's house.

    Summary: At Grandma's and Grandpa's house there
are always special things to see and do.
    [1. Grandparents—Fiction] I. Rosner, Ruth, ill.
II. Title
PZ7.H7654At 1986   [E]   85-15547
ISBN 0-8075-0477-7

At Grandma and Grandpa's house
there are birds and chipmunks
and squirrels,

a doorbell that goes dingdong, dongding,

and Grandma and Grandpa.

There's a light in the front hall closet
that goes on when you open the door
and off when you close it. Once
Grandpa and I stood inside and saw.

In the kitchen there's a drawer full of lots and lots of things

and a cookie jar that looks like a rabbit.

There's a breakfast room with windows all around
and a pair of binoculars you can use if you're careful.

In the bathroom there's a stool
to stand on when you wash
your hands and toys to play with
if you take a bath.

There's a long, long hall for running,

a big bed for bouncing,

and a staying-overnight room

with bunkbeds and toys and trucks and books

and a Swiss village.

There's a place in the living room for blocks and crayons

and games to play with,

and there's a cat named Percy.

In the yard there's a tree to climb

and bushes where the branches make houses to play in.

In the dining room we eat on special plates
and have a tablecloth and candles.

After dinner Grandma tells us stories

and Grandpa fixes my truck.

When we have to leave, we hug and kiss.

"We'll miss you," Grandma and Grandpa say.
"Come back soon!"

"Goodbye, goodbye," we call as we drive away.

Grandma and Grandpa wave even after
we're gone. They told us so.